Hummingbirds

Steven Otfinoski

Cavendish
Square

New York

3 9082 12651 8961

Published in 2015 by Cavendish Square Publishing, LLC
243 5th Avenue, Suite 136, New York, NY 10016

Library of Congress Cataloging-in-Publication Data

Otfinoski, Steven.
Hummingbirds / Steven Otfinoski.
pages cm. — (Backyard safari)
Includes index.
ISBN 978-1-62712-828-5 (hardcover) ISBN 978-1-62712-829-2 (paperback) ISBN 978-1-62712-830-8 (ebook)
1. Hummingbirds—Juvenile literature. I. Title.

QL696.A558O842 2014
598.7'64—dc23

2013047708

Editorial Director: Dean Miller
Editor: Andrew Coddington
Copy Editor: Cynthia Roby
Art Director: Jeffrey Talbot
Designer: Joseph Macri
Photo Researcher: J8 Media
Production Manager: Jennifer Ryder-Talbot
Production Editor: David McNamara

The photographs in this book are used by permission and through the courtesy of: Cover photo by Jean-Luc Baron / Flickr / Getty Images; Minden Pictures /Rufous Hummingbird / Masterfile, 4; Anthony Mercieca / Animals Animals, 5; Robert Lubeck /Animals Animals, 7; Getty Images, 8; Bill Coster / Ardea /Animals Animals 8; Frank Pali / age fotostock / SuperStock, 10; Pat Gaines / Flickr / Getty Images, 12; Mark Caunt / Shutterstock.com, 14; Anthony Mercieca / Animals Animals, 17; Steve Byland / ShutterStock.com, 20; Anthony Mercieca / Photo Researchers / Getty Images, 20; Annie Katz / Photographer's Choice / Getty Images, 21; mmphotos / Stockbyte / Getty Images, 21; James Hager / Robert Harding World Imagery / Getty Images, 21; JIM ZIPP / Photo Researchers / Getty Images, 21; Mariusz S. Jurgielewicz / ShutterStock.com, 25; Straublund Photography / Flickr / Getty Images, 26

Printed in the United States of America

Contents

Introduction

Have you ever watched baby spiders hatch from a silky egg sac, or seen a butterfly sip nectar from a flower? If you have, you know how wonderful it is to discover nature for yourself. Each book in the Backyard Safari series takes you step-by-step on an easy outdoor adventure, and then helps you identify the animals you've found. You'll also learn ways to attract, observe, and protect these valuable creatures. As you read, be on the lookout for the Safari Tips and Trek Talk facts sprinkled throughout the book. Ready? The fun starts just steps from your back door!

ONE
Hummingbird World

Of the thousands of different birds on the planet, few are as amazing as the hummingbird. It is one of the smallest birds and also one of the most extraordinary. Hummingbirds are the only birds that can fly in any direction, even backwards! They are among the most dazzlingly colorful types of birds. Their bright colors gleam in the sunlight. When the light fades, those colors seem to magically change.

This ruby-throated hummingbird is in full flight.

Hummingbirds are also among the fastest flying birds for their size. They can reach speeds up to sixty-five miles (105 kilometers) per hour and are capable of flying long distances. For example, the ruby-throated hummingbird **migrates** each year from the United States to Mexico and South America by crossing the 500-mile- (805-km-) wide Gulf of Mexico. It makes this journey in eighteen to twenty hours nonstop.

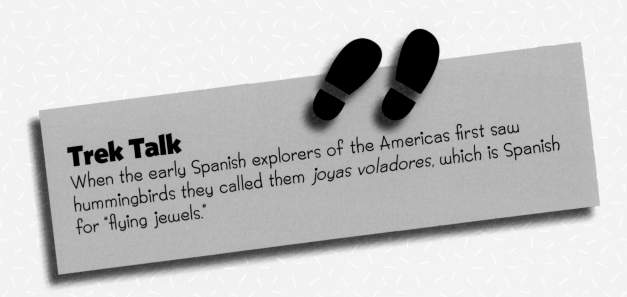

Trek Talk

When the early Spanish explorers of the Americas first saw hummingbirds they called them *joyas voladores*, which is Spanish for "flying jewels."

A Life of Eating

The hummingbird does all this while living an extremely fragile existence. Its **metabolism** is extremely high. Its metabolic rate is 100 times that of an elephant. The hummingbird's tiny heart beats 1,260 times per minute. To fuel its tiny body, the hummingbird must feed constantly. It eats an average of seven times per hour for thirty to sixty seconds each time. If it goes without food for just a few hours, it could die.

To survive through the night, hummingbirds fall into a state of **torpor**. In torpor, the hummingbird's heart rate drops from 1,260 beats per minute to only about fifty beats. Its body temperature also plunges, or drops quickly. A hummingbird in torpor appears to be dead. It wakes from torpor one or two hours before dawn without any outside prompting. During this process, the hummingbird's heart and breathing rates increase. They vibrate their wings to warm up. This series of actions can take up to an hour. And what about those twenty-hour migratory flights? How does the hummingbird survive them? It stores fat in its body when it eats. During the flight it uses up the fat as energy so it doesn't have to eat.

The hummingbird's main diet is the **nectar** it collects from flowers. This sweet plant juice is loaded with sugar that gives the hummingbird lots of energy. It also eats small insects and spiders that it often finds inside the flowers along with the nectar.

Hummingbirds are most attracted to red flowers because they have the sweetest nectar. In return, hummingbirds do a favor for the flowers. Flower **pollen**, like dust, sticks to their needle-like bill

Trek Talk
Hummingbirds consume about 50 percent of their weight in sugar from nectar every day.

and body parts. When they visit another flower, the pollen rubs off their body and onto the new flower. This causes **cross-fertilization.**

High Fliers

Hummingbirds are the daring acrobats of the bird world. They can hover like tiny helicopters above a flower as they eat from it. As they do, they beat their tiny wings back and forth sixty-five to seventy times per second. The humming of the beating wings is what gives the hummingbird its name. Powerful muscles in its wings allow the hummingbird to fly expertly in any direction. Some 30 percent of its body weight is flight muscles.

Hummingbirds can dive at a top speed of sixty-five miles (105 km) per hour and then pull out of the dive just before hitting the ground. When diving, their wings beat up to 200 times per second. Males perform these dazzling dives to scare off other hummingbirds, protect and defend their territory from people and other animals, and impress and attract a female.

Mating and Young

Male and female hummingbirds have a mating ritual that must be seen to be believed. After the male shows off his high-flying acrobatics and attracts a female, both birds will fly upward, facing each other.

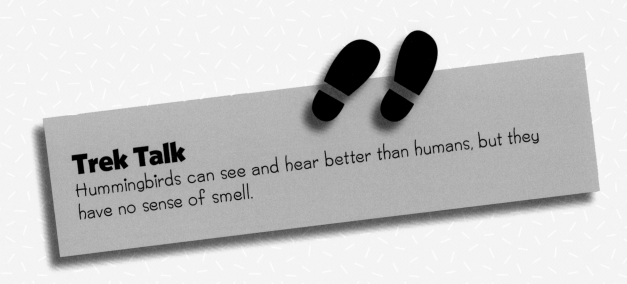

Trek Talk
Hummingbirds can see and hear better than humans, but they have no sense of smell.

A mother hummingbird feeds her chicks beak-to-beak.

Then they may move up and down together or alternatively. They will finally mate.

The male leaves and plays no part in rearing the young. The female is ready to lay her eggs in a matter of days. She is well prepared, having built her nest in the branch of a tree even before finding a mate. The hummingbird's nest is no larger than a half-dollar coin, making it the smallest of all bird nests. The mother makes it out of bark, grass, cattail fluff, and pieces of plant life. She binds the nest together, as well as to the tree branch, with spider webbing. It must be constructed strong and flexible enough to allow the baby hummingbirds to grow in it. She lines the nest with cottonseeds and bird feathers to make it soft.

When they hatch from tiny white eggs, the young, or chicks, are no bigger than a jellybean. Their mother feeds them nectar and insects for about three weeks. After that, the chicks can find their own food. By early fall, they are old enough to fly south on their own.

Most hummingbirds live only three to five years in the wild. In zoos, they can live much longer, sometimes up to ten years.

Trek Talk
The oldest known hummingbird was a broad-tailed hummingbird that lived for twelve years.

A Hummingbird's Body

Only a few hummingbirds are six inches (15 centimeters) or longer in length. The smallest, the bee hummingbird of Cuba, is only two inches (5 cm) in size and weighs one-tenth of an ounce (2.8 grams). The largest hummingbird is the aptly named giant hummingbird. It lives in the Andes Mountains of South America. The giant hummingbird measures 8.25 inches (21 cm) in length and weighs 0.7 ounces (20 g).

The male Anna's hummingbird is known for its bright red head. It lives along the western coast of North America from Canada to Mexico.

More than half of the hummingbird species are found in South America. Ecuador, located along the northwestern coast, boasts 163 species, the largest number of hummingbirds in any one country.

Hummingbirds are covered with bright, **iridescent** feathers. An average-sized hummingbird has 940 feathers. Some are bright green while others are a deep violet or scarlet red. The head, **gorget**, and tail feathers are often the most colorful. The sunlight shining on them causes a dazzling sheen. Hummingbirds have long, needle-thin bills that can easily reach into every corner of a flower blossom. They lap up the nectar with their long tongues in the same way that a cat laps up milk. Their tongues are shaped like the letter 'W' and can shoot out thirteen times per second when eating. Hairs at the tongue's tip help them capture every drop of nectar. The hummingbird's brain makes up 4.2 percent of its body weight. This is the largest proportion of brain-to-body weight in the bird kingdom. Hummingbirds have tiny, weak feet that cannot support them on a flat surface. They prefer to curl their claws around a small tree branch when resting.

There are close to 400 hummingbird **species**, all of which live in the Western **Hemisphere**: North, Central, and South America. The majority of hummingbirds live in Central and South America. Only sixteen species live in the United States and of those, only one, the ruby-throated hummingbird, lives in the eastern United States. Are you ready to go looking for these amazing birds? It's time to go on safari!

Hummingbirds comes in many colors. This blue and green one is resting on a branch between meals.

TWO

You Are the Explorer

The time of year you can find hummingbirds on safari in your backyard depends on where you live. In the eastern and northern regions of the United States you will find them in the daytime from early spring to early fall. In the West and especially the Southwest, you will find them year round. The climate is warmer and does not require them to migrate during the winter months.

What Do I Wear?

- ❋ Light, casual, comfortable clothes
- ❋ If sunny and hot, a hat with a brim
- ❋ Sunglasses
- ❋ Sunscreen

What Do I Take?

- ❋ A pair of binoculars
- ❋ Digital camera
- ❋ Notebook
- ❋ Colored pens or pencils

Where Do I Go?

Hummingbirds will most likely be attracted to these things in your yard:

* Flowers, especially red ones
* Flowering trees, including citrus trees
* Wooded areas
* Grassy areas

If your yard doesn't offer several of these features, here are some other safari locations you can try:

* Meadows or fields with wildflowers
* Woodlands
* Public parks

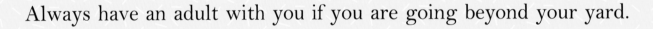

Always have an adult with you if you are going beyond your yard.

What Do I Do?

* Use your binoculars to locate and get a close-up look at any hummingbirds. Be warned. They move very fast through the air, so you'll have to be patient in viewing them. Your best bet is to wait for them near the flowers from which they love to eat—but not too close. You may see them perching on a tree

branch near those flowers. It's one of the few times you'll see them at rest.

❋ Snap a photo with your camera of any hummingbirds you see. Again, you'll have to be fast at taking your picture because of their swift movements.

❋ Make a brief entry in your notebook of every hummingbird sighting, answering questions such as these: What colors are the hummingbird's feathers? What species is it? What is its flight pattern? From what flowers did it feed? Did it also eat any insects that you could see? If you saw more than one hummingbird at one time, how did they respond to one another?

Safari Tip
The trumpet vine is one of the hummingbird's favorite flowering plants. It eats sweet nectar out of the plant's long red-orangish trumpet-shaped blooms.

❋ Using your digital picture as a reference, sketch a drawing of a hummingbird and color it in.

❋ Spend about a half hour to one hour on safari.

❋ Clean up the area and take everything with you when you leave.

How many hummingbirds did you see on your safari? If the answer is none, don't worry. Every safari is different. You are sure to have more success on your next adventure. Plan to go on safari again soon. At home, transfer your photos onto the computer and print them. Share your notebook with a friend or your family. Take someone on safari with you next time. Now it's time to learn more about your backyard visitors!

THREE
A Guide to Hummingbirds

There are 16 species of hummingbirds found in the United States. If you live east of the Mississippi River, you will probably find the ruby-throated hummingbird during your backyard safari. It is the only hummingbird that lives in this part of the country. However, sometimes other species appear east of the Mississippi briefly during periods of migration or by accident. Be on the lookout for them. If you live west of the Mississippi, you can regularly see a number of other species.

While on safari, refer to the hummingbird guide on pages 20-21. Ask yourself these questions to help you use the guide to identify any hummingbird you see in your backyard or other safari location.

* What colors does the hummingbird have on its different body parts, especially its head and gorget?
* How large is its body? Its tail?
* What sounds does it make?
* What is its behavior around other birds? Is it aggressive or more withdrawn?
* What is its flight pattern?

By matching the colors, size, sounds, and other characteristics with the photos in the hummingbird guide, you should be able to identify each hummingbird you see on safari. Here is a sample entry:

Hummingbird Guide

HUMMINGBIRD
Color(s): green (back) black (chin), line of violet below chin
Size: small
Location: hummingbird feeder
Activity: drinking liquid from feeder
Species: black-chinned hummingbird

Ruby-throated Hummingbird

Black-chinned Hummingbird

Rufous Hummingbird

Anna's Hummingbird

Calliope Hummingbird

Costas Hummingbird

FOUR
Try This! Projects You Can Do

Here are a few projects you can do to attract hummingbirds to your backyard and help them when they're in trouble. You'll need an older person or adult to supervise you on some of them.

Create a Liquid Solution for a Hummingbird Feeder

Like many birds, hummingbirds like to eat from human-made birdfeeders. However, while most birds eat solid foods, such as seeds, from feeders, hummingbirds prefer liquid food similar to the nectar they drink from flowers. Making your own feeder can be a complicated process. You will probably find it easier to buy a hummingbird feeder at a local pet store and then prepare and fill it with your own liquid solution. When choosing a hummingbird feeder make sure it has parts that can be easily detached for thorough cleaning.

What Do I Need?

* White sugar
* A small cooking pan
* A hummingbird feeder
* Red ribbon or tape
* A coil of thin metal wire

What Do I Do?

* First, make sure you have adult supervision.
* Mix one part white sugar with four parts tap water in the pan.
* Boil the mixture for three to four minutes on a stovetop.
* Let the solution cool and then fill your feeder with it.

Safari Tip

Do not use honey, artificial sweeteners, or sweet syrups as a substitute for sugar. These substances can become spoiled and produce a mold that can seriously harm hummingbirds. Also, don't add artificial red dye to your mixture. Chemicals can harm hummingbirds, too. The red ribbon or tape wrapped around your feeder will be enough color to attract them.

* Store any remaining solution in the refrigerator. It will stay fresh for up to two weeks and can be used to refill your feeder.
* Unless your feeder is already red in color, wrap the ribbon or tape around it. Red is the color that most attracts hummingbirds.
* Wrap one end of the wire around the feeder, and securely attach the other end to the branch of a tree. Pick a branch near a window of your house so you can observe the hummingbirds up close from inside as they visit your feeder.

Safari Tip

Ants, bees, and wasps may also be attracted to the sugary solution in your hummingbird feeder. To keep them away, try applying a small amount of cooking oil or mineral oil on your fingertip, and then rubbing it around the edges of the feeder hole. This will make it slippery for insects and discourage them from going inside.

Place your feeder outside in early spring and leave it up until early fall. If you live in the western part of the United States, especially the southwest region, you may leave it out all year long. Most hummingbirds remain in that area throughout the year. Clean your feeder every three or four days and replace the liquid. Wash it in hot water and vinegar, and rinse it thoroughly. A dirty feeder will lead to the growth of bacteria. It can cause your solution to become spoiled.

Don't be disappointed if hummingbirds don't immediately show up at your feeder. It may take time for them to find it. You may first place your feeder near any flowers in your backyard. The hummingbirds will be attracted to the flowers and will then see the feeder. Once the birds are familiar with the feeder and begin visiting it regularly, you can move it closer to your house. Then you can watch them through a window.

Your hummingbird feeder may also attract other birds. If it gets too crowded and other birds drive the hummingbirds away, you may want to put up more feeders so there is enough food for every bird that visits your backyard.

Make A Hummingbird Garden

Nectar from flowers is the first dining choice for hummingbirds. You can make a flower garden in your backyard that will attract as many hummingbirds as any feeder.

What Do I Need?

* A shovel or small garden spade
* Various flowers from a garden store
* A small backyard plot or flowerbed, preferably near your house
* Fertilizer
* A garden hose or watering can

What Do I Do?

❋ Pick one area of your backyard to be your hummingbird garden. It may be an already-established flowerbed or a grassy area that you will have to prepare by turning over the soil with a shovel.

❋ Go to your neighborhood garden store with an adult and buy a variety of flowers that produce nectar and have bright colors that will attract hummingbirds. Here are some hummingbird favorites: trumpet vine, dahlias, fuchsia, hibiscus, nasturtium, petunias, Sweet William, and zinnias.

❋ Plant the flowers in your garden. Feed the soil with fertilizer to promote growth. Water the flowers regularly.

❋ If planting in the ground isn't practical where you live, then plant the flowers in hanging pots on a deck, patio, or in a flower box outside a window.

❋ Watch the hummingbirds gather and feed in your hummingbird garden as your flowers bloom.

Use the same notebook you used to record your observations while on safari as you observe hummingbirds at your feeder and in your garden. Think about recording answers to these questions as you watch hummingbirds feed in your backyard:

* What kinds of hummingbirds have been attracted to my backyard?
* Where do more of them gather—at my feeder or in my flower garden?
* What behavior do I observe the hummingbirds exhibiting as they compete for food?
* How long, on average, does a hummingbird spend eating at a flower or feeder? How frequently does it return?
* What other birds are attracted to my feeder or flowers?
* Which flower is most popular among the hummingbirds?

Safari Tip
If you live in a warm climate with mild winters, you may want to make flowering trees a part of your hummingbird garden. The blooms of flowering quince, horse chestnut, and citrus trees all attract hummingbirds.

Enjoy watching these amazing little birds dart, fly, and feed in your backyard. They will make for an especially colorful and exciting safari!

Glossary

cross-fertilization the fertilization of one plant by the reproductive cells of another related plant

gorget a part of the throat on a bird that stands out for its color and texture

hemisphere one of the halves that the world's land mass is divided into

iridescent displaying very bright, changing colors

metabolism the processes by which a body breaks down food and converts it to energy

migrate to move from one place to another; in the case of animals and birds, to a warmer location

nectar the sweet secretions of a plant on which hummingbirds and other birds feed

pollen the fertilizing parts of plants, composed of fine, powdery grains

species one type of animal or plant within a larger category

torpor a trance-like state of inactivity entered by some animals and birds to conserve energy

Find Out More

Books

Bogue, Gary. *There's a Hummingbird in My Backyard.* Berkeley, CA: Heyday Books, 2010.

Larson, Jeanette. *Hummingbirds: Facts and Folklore from the Americas.* Watertown, MA: Charlesbridge Publishing, 2011.

Sill, Cathryn, and John Sill. *About Hummingbirds: A Guide for Children.* (The About Series). Atlanta, GA: Peachtree Publishers, 2011.

Swanson, Diane. *Hummingbirds. Welcome to the World Series.* Vancouver, BC, Canada: Whitecap Books, 2010.

Websites

Hummingbirds

www.kidcyber.com.au/topics/hummingbird.htm

Learn many fascinating facts about hummingbirds and follow a link to a hummingbird video.

Fact Sheet: Hummingbirds

www.defenders.org/hummingbirds/basic-facts

Learn about the hummingbirds' diet, range, behavior, and conservation efforts to save them.

Anna's Hummingbird

kids.sandiegozoo.org/animals/birds/annas-hummingbird

Find out all about this popular species of hummingbird and view lots of great photos.

Index

Page numbers in **boldface** are illustrations.

About the Author

STEVEN OTFINOSKI has written more than 160 books for young readers, many of them about animals, ranging from koalas to scorpions. Growing up, his pets included turtles, cats, and dogs. He lives in Connecticut with his wife, their daughter, and two dogs.